R0201352473

08/2020

THE
SPRING DANCE
FROM THE
BLACK LAGOON

Get more monster-sized laughs from

The Black Lagoon:

THE
SPRING DANCE
FROM THE
BLACK LAGOON

WOULD YOU LIKE TO DANCE?

SURE, BUT DON'T STEP ON MY TOES.

by Mike Thaler
Illustrated by Jared Lee

SCHOLASTIC INC.

New York   Toronto   London   Auckland   Sydney
Mexico City   New Delhi   Hong Kong   Buenos Aires

visit us at www.abdopublishing.com

Reinforced library bound edition published in 2012 by Spotlight, a division of the ABDO Group, PO Box 398166, Minneapolis, MN 55439. Spotlight produces high-quality reinforced library bound editions for schools and libraries. Published by agreement with Scholastic Inc.
Printed in the United States of America, North Mankato, Minnesota.
102011
122012

This book contains at least 10% recycled materials.

To Jean & Jack, Bethanne & Scott Hernia Heroes —M.T.
To Cheryl Emmerich —J.L.

Library of Congress Cataloging-in-Publication Data

This book was previously cataloged with the following information:

Thaler, Mike, 1936-
  The spring dance from the black lagoon / by Mike Thaler ; illustrated by Jared Lee.
    p.   cm. – (Black Lagoon Adventures, bk. 15)
Series: Black Lagoon adventures
[1. Dance parties—Juvenile fiction. 2. Dance parties —fiction.]
PZ7.T3 Sp 2009
[E] – dc22

2011380749

ISBN 978-1-59961-963-7 (reinforced library edition)

HAPPY STAR →

All Spotlight books are reinforced library bindings and manufactured in the United States of America.

CONTENTS

CHAPTER 1
A BLOOMIN' DISASTER

It's spring! The flowers are blooming, the birds are singing, and our class is having a dance. We all have to go. And we all have to dance . . . with the *girls*!

GIRL → HIPPO

I LOVE SPRING.

A spring dance—this is going to be a disaster. I know how to spring, but I don't know how to dance. The only steps I know are how to step on other people's feet. Mrs. Green says it'll be lots of fun, but I know it'll be for the birds.

THE SPRING DANCE WILL BE WONDERFUL.

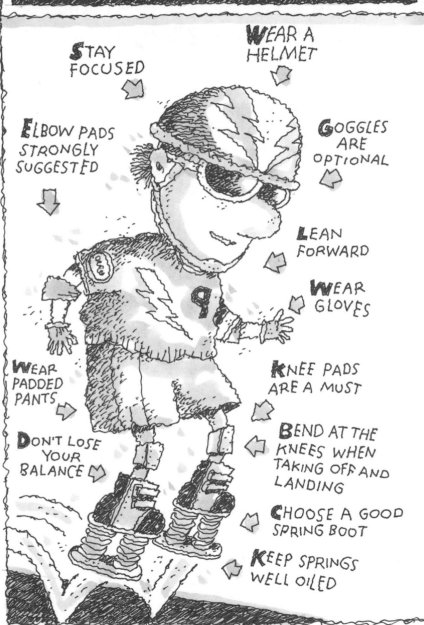

CHAPTER 2
TEASE FOR TWO

On the school bus, the girls are giggling and the boys are grumbling.

"Hey, Hubie, save a dance for me!" shouts Penny. Then they all giggle when my ears turn red.

How is it that girls know just how to torture you?

"Hey, Hubie, are you going to wear a tuxedo?" yells Eric.

Boys can torture pretty well, too.

ERIC

BLACK TIE →

WHITE DINNER JACKET

PINK CUMMERBUND

BLACK PANTS →

BLACK SOCKS

WHITE SHOES →

HUBIE'S TUXEDO

For the next ten blocks it's Pick on Hubie Day.

Everyone gets into the act. And when I finally get off the bus, my ears are as red as a fire engine.

CHAPTER 3
OUT OF THE FRYING PAN

I go straight to my room and slam the door. Mom comes in.

"What's wrong, Hubie?"

"Nothing."

"Come on, Hubie, your ears are on fire—what's bothering you?"

I bare my soul. "It's the dance, Mom. This Friday, in school, with *girls*."

"Well, what's so bad about that?"

"First of all, I'm clumsy."

"You can practice."

OOPS!

#1

TRIP!

18

"Secondly, I have two left feet."
"We can operate."
"And thirdly . . . I don't know how to dance."

19

"No problem. Get in the car. I'll take you to dance class."

Oh, no, why don't I learn to keep my mouth shut? Every time I tell my mom a problem, I wind up with two more.

21

CHAPTER 4
NO CLASS

We pull up in front of Mrs. Tunny's dance studio. The sign on the door says, WALK IN AND DANCE OUT. Mom takes me by the arm and leads me in. Well, *drags* me in would be more accurate.

MOM, I THINK I HAVE A FEVER.

TUNNY'S DANCE STUDIO

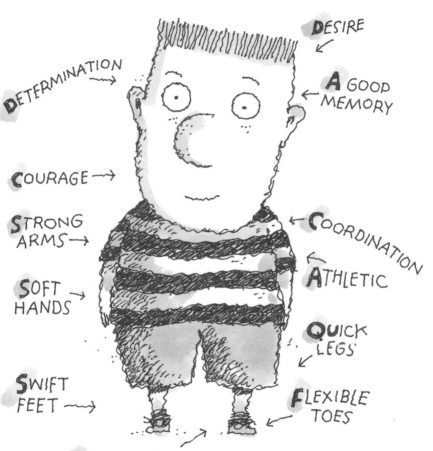

WHAT IT TAKES TO BE A GOOD DANCER *

DESIRE

DETERMINATION →

A GOOD MEMORY

COURAGE →

STRONG ARMS →

SOFT HANDS →

SWIFT FEET →

COORDINATION

ATHLETIC

QUICK LEGS

FLEXIBLE TOES

THE ABILITY TO MOVE YOUR FEET ACROSS THE FLOOR WITHOUT TOUCHING THE FLOOR.

* NONE OF THESE CHARACTERISTICS APPLY TO HUBIE.

23

I hope none of my friends see me here. Oh, no, they're all here— Eric, Derek, Freddy, and Randy. They've been *dragged* in, too. It's amazing how all our moms think alike.

25

CHAPTER 5
TRIPPING THE LIGHT FANTASTIC

NFL
LINEBACKER

Mrs. Tunny is a linebacker. She bounces over and grabs my hand. Then she hauls me to the center of the room.

YOU'RE THROWING THE WRONG KIND OF BALL.

OOPS.

"I will now demonstrate the tango," she shouts over the music.

YO-YO →

She twirls me, spins me, pulls me, rolls me, and throws me. Dancing's rough—it's more like a *tangle*. I feel like a yo-yo. When I unwind, she grabs me again.

Everything's dark. I can't hear the music. I can barely breathe. Dancing is dangerous. After an hour of torture to tunes, class is over. We all limp out.

"See you next week!" Mrs. Tunny shouts.

No way. I'd rather wrestle a sumo or box with an octopus.

CHAPTER 6
OKEY DOKEY

When I get home, Mom gives me a few tips about dips. I already learned the tangle. Then there's the cha-cha. If I train for that, I'll have a cha-cha train. Then there's the can-can. I don't think I can-can do that.

34

I might manage the bunny hop, but forget the bossa nova, the hula-hula, and the hokey-pokey. I wonder if there's a hoopy-poopy? I'm just not cut out for this.

I'm way too square. Hey, maybe
I can do a *square* dance.

CHAPTER 7
PICTURE PERFECT

That night I watch lots of dance movies on TV.

Fred Astaire and Gene Kelly—boy, those guys could dance. They had flying feet that caught the beat. I grab the lamp and try a few steps around the living room.

FRED ASTAIRE

GINGER ROGERS, FRED'S DANCING PARTNER

WINGS

TAP TAP TAP TAP TAP TAP TAP

39

DIDN'T I SEE YOU ON PAGE 26.

I don't trip the light fantastic—I just trip over the light. I'm afraid I'm hopeless and hopless.

I have clods that plod.

MRS. TUNNY'S EVALUATION OF HUBIE'S FIRST (AND LAST) DANCING LESSON

I LOVE JELL-O.

CHAPTER 8
HELLO, JELL-O

That night I have a dancemare. I'm wearing 200-pound shoes and I'm trying to dance on Jell-O. The dance is a jitterbug. I have the jitters and I try to bug them out, but I just sink deeper in the Jell-O. It's lemon-lime. At least it's a flavor I like.

THE END.

BLACK LAGOON

Z

Z

Z

CHAPTER 9

GETTING IN STEP

PLEASE DON'T BEND THE PAGES, HUBIE.

OK.

ONE STEP AT A TIME

The next day at school, I go to the library. Mrs. Beamster has a book on how to dance. It's called *One Step at a Time*. It has little footprints showing how to move.

I follow the diagrams and move my feet under the table.

"Stop fidgeting, Hubie," she says.

"I'm not, Mrs. Beamster, I'm dancing."

45

"Hubie, the library is not the place for you to practice the terpsichorean arts." I don't know what the twerp-scorpion arts are . . . but if I had eight legs, I'd need a lot more practice.

ONE, TWO, THREE...
ONE, TWO, FIVE...
ONE, THREE, SEVEN...

COOL.

YOU'RE NOT KEEPING IN STEP, HUBIE.

I go to the boys' bathroom. There's no one there, so I do my moves in the mirror. I think I have the box step just about down. I'm flushed with excitement!

47

CHAPTER 10
ALL WASHED UP

It's Friday. The big day! I get up early and take an hour shower. Then I put on lots of underarm deodorant. It's the pits, but I smell like a flower. Next, I check for pimples. That zit!

• ← PIMPLE

When you dance with girls, they are very close to you. They see everything. They smell everything. I brush my teeth three times and gargle with Mom's mouthwash. I'm as ready as I'll ever be.

49

SCRAPPY CHARACTER →

CHAPTER 11
FRIDAY FEVER

On the school bus, the girls have on pretty dresses and shiny shoes. I hope I don't wind up

stepping on any. The girls smell good, too.

We all get through the day and at two o'clock we go to the gym. It's decorated with spring things like birds, flowers, trees, and bees. I wish they'd all buzz off. The boys line up on one side and the girls on the other.

The music starts and we just stare at each other. Someone's got to break the ice. It might as well be me.

CHAPTER 12
CROSSING THE GREAT DIVIDE

I start across the floor. Everyone's looking at me. What if I trip? What if I fall? What if no one will dance with me? Humiliation!

I KNEW HUBIE WOULD BE THE FIRST TO COME OVER.

MY HERO.

MY KNIGHT IN SHINING ARMOR.

THE LEADER OF THE PACK.

THE KING OF HEARTS.

I'm getting closer to the girls. They're looking at me. Then Doris smiles. I take her hand and lead her out onto the dance floor.

HELLO, KIDS!

I'M HAPPY!

CHAPTER 13
HAVING A BALL

The music is a boogie-woogie. Sounds like something you'd find in your nose. I just stand, holding her hand, and we stare at each other.

BOOGIE-WHAT?

WHAT'S A BOOGIE-WOOGIE?

Everybody's watching. Move, legs, move!

HUBIE'S JUST STANDING THERE.

I start doing the box step with a little wiggle.

Doris does the same. We're dancing! She spins me—I spin her. This is fun!

The music ends way too soon—I was just getting warmed up. I hope my deodorant holds out.

When the music starts again—
all the girls come up and ask me
to dance.

Instead of being a wallflower, I have my pick of the bouquet. In all fairness, I give out numbers and dance with everyone. Hey, Gene Kelly's got nothing on me . . . I'm footloose and fancy-free!

YOU'RE A GOOD DANCER, NUMBER 7.

I'M NEXT, HUBIE.